DragonBorn
Monster Hunter

BY MICHAEL DAHL
ILLUSTRATED BY LUIGI AIME

STONE ARCH
BOOKS™

ZONE BOOKS ARE PUBLISHED BY
STONE ARCH BOOKS
A CAPSTONE IMPRINT
1710 ROE CREST DRIVE
NORTH MANKATO, MINNESOTA 56003
WWW.CAPSTONEPUB.COM

LIBRARY OF CONGRESS CATALOGING-IN-PUBLICATION DATA
DAHL, MICHAEL.
MONSTER HUNTER / WRITTEN BY MICHAEL DAHL ; ILLUSTRATED BY LUIGI AIME.
P. CM. -- (DRAGONBORN)

SUMMARY: IN TOKYO, REN HAS MET WITH THREE OTHER TEENAGERS WHO HAVE THE DRAGON
BIRTHMARK, BUT THE PUBLIC HAS LEARNED THAT THE DRAGONBORN EXIST AND TEAMS OF
HUNTERS ARE SEARCHING FOR THEM--AND NOT ALL OF REN'S NEW FRIENDS ARE WHAT THEY
SEEM TO BE.

ISBN 978-1-4342-4040-8 [LIBRARY BINDING]
ISBN 978-1-4342-4256-3 [PBK.]
ISBN 978-1-4342-4624-0 [EBOOK]
1. DRAGONS--JUVENILE FICTION. 2. ESCAPES--JUVENILE FICTION. 3. TOKYO [JAPAN]--JUVENILE
FICTION. [1. DRAGONS--FICTION. 2. ESCAPES--FICTION. 3. TOKYO [JAPAN]--FICTION. 4. JAPAN--
FICTION.] I. AIME, LUIGI, ILL. II. TITLE.
PZ7.D15134MM 2012
813.54--DC23   2012004663

ART DIRECTOR: KAY FRASER
GRAPHIC DESIGNER: HILARY WACHOLZ
PRODUCTION SPECIALIST: KATHY MCCOLLEY

PHOTO CREDITS:
SHUTTERSTOCK: CAESART (METAL PLATE, PP. 1, 4, 66); FERNANDO CORTES [DRAGON PATTERN]

PRINTED IN THE UNITED STATES OF AMERICA AT CORPORATE GRAPHICS
IN NORTH MANKATO, MINNESOTA.
102012   007006R

TABLE OF CONTENTS

A NEW AGE OF DRAGONS HAS BEGUN.

DRAGONBORN

Young people around the world
have discovered that dragon blood
flows in their veins. They are filled
with new power and new ideas.
But before they reveal themselves
to the world, they must find one
another . . .

CHAPTER 1
Many Warnings

Ren heard the warning from a TV screen.

He was watching the news while riding the train.

The superfast train was taking him from school to a mall downtown.

"Real monsters," said the news announcer.

"Creatures that look like you or me, but can change in the blink of an eye."

Ren looked around the train car. He was surrounded by a crowd of people.

Were they staring at him?

"These creatures may look like humans. But they are not," the announcer went on. "I know it sounds unbelievable, but doctors have discovered a strange new blood disease. A disease that comes from lizards."

A man standing next to Ren nodded his head. He was also watching the TV.

The man turned to his friends. They were young businessmen in suits, carrying briefcases.

"It's about the monsters," the man said.

"They're dangerous," said one of the other businessmen.

"They killed an old woman in my neighborhood," said another. "I heard it on the news."

"And I heard they eat small children," added a third.

Ren felt hot.

The men's talk was making him angry.

But he had to be careful. He had to control his emotions.

Ren knew that whenever strong feelings flooded through him, he started to change.

The train suddenly slowed down.

Ren bumped into one of the businessmen.

The man frowned and looked down at Ren.

"Sorry," said Ren.

The TV news announcer continued. "The creatures are easy to identify. Each one has a strange birthmark on its body."

Ren realized he was rubbing his arm.

It was the arm with the birthmark.

Did the men on the train know what he was hiding?

The businessman was still staring down at Ren.

He had an odd look on his face.

"What's wrong with your eyes?" asked the man.

Ren stared back at the man.

In the man's glasses, Ren could see a reflection of his own eyes.

They were turning yellow.

They looked like lizard's eyes.

The train stopped.

Quickly, Ren jumped off.

He looked back as the train doors hissed shut.

He saw the businessmen through the windows. They were still talking.

Then one of them turned and pointed at Ren.

They knew.

CHAPTER 2
Secret Companions

"Hey, you!" someone shouted.

Ren turned and froze.

He saw a dragon.

A giant poster covered one wall of the
train station.

The poster displayed an evil-looking dragon.

It had red wings and was spitting fire.

Words on the poster read:

THEY ARE EVERYWHERE

いたるところにあり

THEY ARE EVERYWHERE

モンスター

More words read:

IF YOU SUSPECT ANYONE OF BEING A
DANGER, CALL THE POLICE

"You! Hey!" came a shout.

A teenage boy, the same age as Ren, ran up to him.

"Are you Ren?" the boy asked. Then, with a shy smile, he added, "I'm Kazu."

Ren nodded nervously. "I think someone on the train knew me," he said. "I mean, they knew what I was."

Kazu looked at Ren's jacket.

"But your arms are covered," Kazu said. "No one would see. Let's go get something to eat."

The two boys hurried along toward a huge mall.

"The food court's over there," said Kazu.

"I need to stop at the cash machine," said Ren.

"Look," said Kazu. "There they are."

Ren saw two strangers walking toward them, a boy and a girl.

"I'm Hiro," said the boy. "And this is Aya," he added, pointing at the girl.

"I can speak for myself," said Aya.

She smiled at Ren, and he smiled back.

"Is this the first time any of us have met each other?" Aya asked.

They all nodded.

Ren had chatted online with each of them. They had found one another through a special website.

This was the first day they met in person. They had to.

It was getting dangerous to be them. They had to band together.

"My school was having a special inspection," Ren said, walking next to Aya. "The nurse was going to look at every student, and check for birthmarks."

"My school, too," said Hiro.

He looked at the others. "I don't know what I'll tell my parents. How can I go back home now?"

Aya stopped walking. "I hate that!" she snapped.

A dragon poster hung above their heads. "That's so unfair," she said.

"Quiet," said Kazu. "You'll get us in trouble."

"Where's Yoko?" Ren asked.

"Don't worry," said Kazu. "She is meeting us there."

A horrible scream ripped through the air.

Then the young people heard someone shout: "The monster! The monster!"

The scream came from the food court.

CHAPTER 3
The Hunters

"Yoko!" shouted Aya.

Ren and the others rushed down some stairs.

They could see a girl. She stood in the center of the food court.

A mob of people surrounded her in a wide circle.

A young boy was crying, pointing at her. "She has monster eyes!" he wailed.

"No! No, I don't!" said the girl.

Two police officers walked up to the girl.

Ren watched them grab her arms.

"That is Yoko," said Aya. "She told us she'd be carrying a yellow bag."

"Not so loud," said Kazu. "We can't let people know we know her."

"We have to help her," said Aya.

But how? wondered Ren.

"If we try to help her, then the hunters will grab us too," said Hiro.

Ren felt the birthmark on his arm begin to burn.

If he transformed here, and people saw what he was, then what would happen? He thought about the dragon posters. *Danger.*

"Oh no!" said Hiro.

The two police officers stepped back quickly from Yoko.

She seems taller, thought Ren.

She *was* taller.

Higher and higher the girl grew.

Two huge wings unfolded from her shoulders.

Someone in the crowd screamed.

Someone else threw a food tray.

The crowd scattered in fear as the girl dragon rose into the air.

The dragon's wings flapped loudly.

The rush of air knocked over chairs and tables. Potted plants rolled on the floor.

Ren looked up.

There was no way for the dragon to escape. The ceiling was covered with thick glass and metal tubes.

"She can't get out," Ren said to Hiro.

The dragon screamed.

She lowered her scaly jaws and opened her mouth wide.

A stream of fire shot toward the floor.

Before Ren could move, three men pushed past him.

They wore uniforms with dark helmets.

Each of them held a strange weapon.

As the men ran, they surrounded the rising dragon.

"Look!" shouted a young woman. "It's the monster hunters!"

One of the men made a sharp gesture with his hand.

Then all three of them raised their weapons.

The dragon roared.

The weapons fired.

Dark metal nets shot out at the creature.

The dragon tried to fly away, but it was too late.

The nets had done their work. They weighed down the creature's wings.

"That's what could happen to us," Hiro said softly.

The creature sank back to the floor of the food court.

More men in uniforms ran out of the shadows.

"We have to get out of here," whispered Kazu.

"This way," said Aya.

CHAPTER 4
Hiding

A few moments later, the four teenagers were outside the mall.

Lightning flashed in the sky.

They hid in an alleyway.

They crouched down behind trash bins.

"Now what do we do?" asked Hiro.

"We can't go home."

"Why not?" asked Kazu.

Hiro pulled off his jacket. "Because of this," he said.

He showed his bare arm to the others.

They looked at his dragon-shaped birthmark.

Ren pulled off his jacket and revealed his own mark.

Then Kazu did, and then Aya.

"We're all the same," said Ren. "The same as Yoko. That's why we have to stick together."

Lightning flashed again in the sky.

Hiro grinned. "Maybe we should all change," he said. "And fly out of here."

Aya shook her head. "Someone would see us," she said.

"I can fly fast," Hiro said.

"Those net guns were pretty fast, too," said Aya.

"I'm not very good at flying," said Kazu. He stared up at the sky.

"I could help you," Ren said. "We all could."

Aya stood up. "No, she said. "We have to find a place to hide."

A siren sounded nearby.

Ren stood up next to Aya. "I think we better go now," he said.

CHAPTER 5
On the Run

The sirens grew louder.

"It's the hunters," said Ren.

They ran down the alley. "Now where?" said Hiro.

Aya led them down another alley.

The sky grew dark above them.

Streetlights blinked on along the streets. The group saw dark vans speeding through the streets.

When the vans stopped, crews of men jumped out.

The men wore uniforms and carried weapons.

The four dragonteens stayed in the shadows.

When they reached busy streets, they tried to blend in with the walking crowds.

They didn't want anyone to notice them.

They came to a big, busy intersection. Vans were parked everywhere.

Bright streetlights and neon signs lit up the night.

"I don't like it here," whispered Hiro. "Where exactly are we going?"

"Here!" shouted Aya. She shouted again. "Here! Over here!" She waved her arms above her head.

It's a trap! thought Ren. "What are you doing?" he cried.

Aya turned and looked at the others. "Freaks!" she said. "You're monsters. You're not human."

"But you're one of us," said Ren.

"I *was* one of you," said Aya. "But then I was cured. The doctors helped me. And that's what they'll do with you, if they decide not to destroy you."

The hunters were coming closer.

"No!" shouted Hiro.

He raised his arms in the air and groaned. His body thickened and grew larger. Dark wings sprang out from his shoulders.

The monster hunters ran toward him and raised their weapons.

Kazu gripped Ren's shoulder. "We have to go!" he said.

Hiro had disappeared, and the dragon stood in his place. The creature lifted its mighty head. Flames shot from between rows of fangs.

A van caught on fire. A dozen hunters surrounded the monster.

"Now!" shouted their leader.

Metal nets wrapped tightly around the dragon's huge body.

The creature spun around and around. It tried to escape the netting.

Its sharp wings tore through some of the metal strands. "Look out!" yelled one of the hunters.

More hunters appeared. They shot net after net at the creature.

The dragon roared in frustration.

CHAPTER 6
Falling Rain

Aya turned and pointed.

"There's two more!" she yelled. "Don't let them get away."

The two boys ran.

Rain poured down on the city streets.

Kazu ran like a deer, and Ren followed close behind.

They soon reached a park in the middle of the city. They rushed into the bushes.

Ren's lungs felt like fire. "Wait, wait," he said, panting. "Maybe we should do what Hiro said. Maybe we should fly out of here."

Kazu looked up at the dark sky. Rain poured onto his face.

"Don't be scared," said Ren. "I'll help."

"But —" said Kazu.

Then Ren saw it. Rain flowed down Kazu's arm.

His dragon birthmark was washing away.

Another trap!

"You!" cried Ren.

Kazu shook his head. "No. I'm not like Aya," he said. "I've always liked dragons. They're noble. They're powerful. My brother is one, and I always wanted to be like him. But I'm not."

"I don't understand," said Ren.

"I went on the website to help," Kazu said. "To help people like my brother." He smiled. "You can come home with me," he said. "My family knows about my brother, and they don't care. You'll find a safe place there."

Ren thought hard.

There was nowhere else to go.

Moments later, the lightning flashes revealed a dragon rising from the city park.

And from the monster's claws hung a wide-eyed teenage boy.

AUTHOR

Michael Dahl is the author of more than 200 books for children and young adults. He has won the AEP Distinguished Achievement Award three times for his nonfiction. His Finnegan Zwake mystery series was shortlisted twice by the Anthony and Agatha awards. He has also written the Dragonblood series. He is a featured speaker at conferences around the country on graphic novels and high-interest books for boys.

ILLUSTRATOR

Luigi Aime was born in 1987 in Savigliano, a small Italian city near Turin. Even when he was only three years old, he loved to draw. He attended art school, graduating with honors in Illustration and Animation from the European Institute of Design in Milan, Italy.

DISCUSSION QUESTIONS

1. Why did Aya, Ren, Kazu, and Hiro meet?

2. Why were people with dragonblood being hunted?

3. What questions do you still have about this story? Discuss them!

WRITING PROMPTS

1. What happens after this book ends? Write a short story that extends the book.

2. It can be very interesting to think about a story from another person's point of view. Try writing this story, or part of it, from Aya's point of view. What does she see, hear, think, and say? What does she notice? How is the story different?

3. Create a cover for a book. It can be this book or another book you like, or a made-up book. Write the information on the back, and include the author and illustrator names.

GLOSSARY

band (BAND)—join together

birthmark (BURTH-mark)—a mark that is present at birth

gesture (JESS-chur)—an action that communicates an idea or feeling

identify (eye-DEN-tuh-fye)—to recognize or tell what something is or who someone is

mob (MOB)—a large group of people

noble (NOH-buhl)—impressive or magnificent in appearance

reflection (ri-FLEK-shuhn)—an image seen in a shiny surface, like a mirror

revealed (ri-VEELD)—showed or brought into view

surrounded (suh-ROUND-id)—grouped around something

unbelievable (uhn-bi-LEEV-uh-buhl)—hard to accept as true

THEY MUST WORK TOGETHER TO
FIGHT THE COMING BATTLE. BUT FIRST
THEY MUST FIND EACH OTHER ...

REN YAMAMOTO

Ren was bullied by a group of boys one afternoon after school. When he got home, he washed his face in the pond in his family's garden. His reflection was not human. Since then, he has been more afraid of himself than of anyone — or anything — else.

Age: 16
Hometown: Tokyo, Japan
Dragon appearance: Blue and black
Dragon species: *Draconis potentia* ("power dragon")
Strength: Super-powerful wings

DRAGONBLOOD
RUNS THROUGH THEIR VEINS...

Find cool websites and more books like this one
at www.Facthound.com.